LITTLE RED RIDING HOOD

Dedicated To:
Our Children

A Special Thanks To:
Stacy and her Mother
Pomper
Dick
Andy
and
Del

LITTLE RED RIDING HOOD
French and German Folklore

1st Edition 1985
Illustrations Copyright © 1985 by Shirley Holt
Text copyright © ShirLee Publications, Lee Richardson
All rights reserved under Pan-American Copyright Convention. Printed in the
United States by Herald Printers. Binding by Hiller, Salt Lake City.
Typography by Monterey Graphics

ShirLee Publications, Post Office Box 22122,
Carmel, California 93922
ISBN 0-9613476-1-9

LITTLE RED RIDING HOOD

Illustrated By
SHIRLEY HOLT

Retold By
LEE RICHARDSON

Once there was a little girl
who lived with her mother in
a house on the edge of a dense
forest.

One morning her mother filled
a basket with some fresh apple
tarts, a tin of peppermint tea
and six brown eggs.

"Take this food to Grandmother,"
she told the little girl.
"Grandmother is very sick.
These good things to eat
will help her to get well."

Grandmother's cottage lay deep
within the forest.
The little girl's mother said,
"Take the path through the forest.
T'is the quickest way.
Be sure to stay on the path,
or you might get lost.
Remember," she said, shaking her
finger, "go straight there.
Do not stop along the way."

The little girl hugged her mother
and said, "I promise."
She put on her favorite red cloak
and hood that Grandmother had made
for her.
Then she picked up the basket and
walked down the path that led through
the forest to Grandmother's cottage.

The little girl soon forgot
her promise when she saw an
owl sitting in a tree.
"Who are you?" he asked.

"Everyone calls me Red Riding
Hood," she said.

"Be on your way, Little Red
Riding Hood," said the owl.
"A big mean wolf lives in this
forest.
He has not eaten in three days
and is very hungry.
He could swallow a little girl
like you in one mouthful!"

Red Riding Hood shivered as she
thought of the wolf.
She pulled her cloak tighter around
her and hurried down the path.

It was not long before she stopped again to pick some pretty daisies.

Suddenly, out jumped the wolf!
"Good morning, Little Red Riding
Hood," he said.
"Where are you going on this fine day?"

"To my grandmother's," she said.
He seemed so friendly that she
was not afraid of him.

"Where does your grandmother live?"

"In the stone cottage at the end
of the path," said Red Riding Hood.

"Why not take some wild berries to
her?" said the sly wolf.
"There are some big, red, juicy ones
growing just beyond the tall fir tree."

"Thank you, Wolf," she said. "I will.
Grandmother likes to eat berries for
her breakfast."

While Red Riding Hood went to
look for the berry patch, the
wolf ran ahead to Grandmother's
cottage.

"How clever I have been," thought
the wolf.
"Now I shall eat both of them for
my supper!"
He remembered how tender and plump
Red Riding Hood had looked.
"I shall eat her first!" grinned
the wolf.
His mouth began to water at the
thought of eating such a delicious
meal.

When the wolf arrived at the
cottage he knocked on the door.

"Who is there?" called Grandmother
from her bed.

"Little Red Riding Hood," said the
wolf in a tiny voice.

"Lift the latch and walk in, my
dear," said Grandmother.

The wolf lifted the latch and the
door swung open.
He ran to the bed and grabbed up
the little old lady.
He quickly pushed her into the closet
and locked the door.
The wolf wrapped Grandmother's shawl
around his shoulders and over his head.
He placed her glasses gently on his nose.
Then he leaped into her bed, pulled the
quilt under his chin and waited
for Red Riding Hood to come.

Red Riding Hood picked some
wild berries and tucked them in around
the edge of the basket.
Then she suddenly remembered the
promise she had made to her mother
and ran straight away to Grandmother's
cottage.

"How strange," she thought.
"The door is open!"
She peeked around the door and
called, "Grandmother, I have
brought some special treats for you."

Grandmother did not answer.
"Where can she be?" thought Red
Riding Hood.
"Maybe she is sleeping."
She tiptoed to Grandmother's bed.

"Good morning, Grandmother,"
said Red Riding Hood.
"Are you feeling better?"

The wolf nodded his head, and the shawl
fell away from his face.
"Come closer, my dear," he said.

"Grandmother, what big ears you have!"

"All the better to hear you with, my dear."

"Grandmother, what big eyes you have!"

"All the better to see you with, my dear."

"Grandmother, what big hands you have!"

"All the better to hold you with, my dear."

"If you are my grandmother why are your
teeth so long and sharp?"

"All the better to eat you with,
my dear!" snarled the hungry wolf.
With that he leaped out of the bed
and grabbed Little Red Riding Hood!

At first she was so frightened that
she could not move.
Then she kicked him as hard as she
could and he let go of her.
She ran to the window.
"Help! Help!" she called.
"Someone please help me!"

The wolf smiled and showed his long
sharp teeth.
"No one can help you now," he chuckled.
Then he grabbed her again!
"Little Red Riding Hood," he said.
"You are to be my supper!"

Nearby in the forest a hunter was
chasing a gray fox.
He heard Red Riding Hood's cries for
help.
He ran to the little stone cottage.

'You old sinner!" shouted
the hunter when he saw the wolf.
"This is the end of you!"
As he raised his gun to shoot,
the wolf slipped out the door.
Before the hunter could get off a shot,
the wolf disappeared into the forest
and was never seen again.

"Let me out! Let me out!"
Red Riding Hood hurried to the closet.
She unlocked the door and let
Grandmother out.
They thanked the hunter for saving them
from the hungry wolf and invited him to
stay for tea.

"I want to find the gray fox before the sun
goes down," he said.
"So I must hurry."
He turned and walked back into the forest.

Grandmother took two cups out of
the cupboard and set them on the table.
She reached into the basket for some
apple tarts.
She poured Red Riding Hood a nice hot
cup of peppermint tea and one for
herself.

Soon Grandmother's cheeks were rosy
and her eyes began to twinkle.
"My goodness," she said.
"I am feeling better already."

Suddenly, the clock struck three.
"Bong! Bong! Bong!"
"Oh dear," said Red Riding Hood, "it
is time for me to leave."

She kissed her grandmother and said,
"I will come again tomorrow.
Do not worry, Grandmother.
Next time I will keep my promise.
I will never stop along the way again."
Then she picked up the empty basket,
waved goodbye and walked straight down
the path to her home.

THE END